Triggered

Vicki Grant

orca soundings

ORCA BOOK PUBLISHERS

Library and Archives Canada Cataloguing in Publication

Grant, Vicki, author
Triggered / Vicki Grant.
(Orca soundings)

Issued in print and electronic formats.
ISBN 978-1-4598-0529-3 (bound).--ISBN 978-1-4598-0526-2 (pbk.)
ISBN 978-1-4598-0527-9 (pdf).--ISBN 978-1-4598-0528-6 (epub)

I. Title. II. Series: Orca soundings
PS8613.R367T75 2013   jc813'.6   C2013-902341-0
C2013-902342-9

First published in the United States, 2013
Library of Congress Control Number: 2013906261

Summary: After Mick breaks up with Jade, his sense of responsibility for her
younger brother keeps pulling him back.

MIX
Paper from
responsible sources
FSC® C016245
www.fsc.org

*Orca Book Publishers is dedicated to preserving the environment and has
printed this book on Forest Stewardship Council® certified paper.*

Orca Book Publishers gratefully acknowledges the support for its publishing
programs provided by the following agencies: the Government of Canada through
the Canada Book Fund and the Canada Council for the Arts,
and the Province of British Columbia through the BC Arts Council
and the Book Publishing Tax Credit.

Cover image by Masterfile

ORCA BOOK PUBLISHERS
PO Box 5626, Stn. B
Victoria, BC Canada
V8R 6S4

ORCA BOOK PUBLISHERS
PO Box 468
Custer, WA USA
98240-0468

www.orcabook.com
Printed and bound in Canada.

16 15 14 13 • 4 3 2 1

Mick

Chapter One

We're alone. Jade's mother is working the night shift. Her little brother's in bed. If I'm going to say anything, now's the time.

I close the window on my desktop. I stare at the blank screen and run the words through my head again. I thought I had it all worked out, but I'm not so sure anymore.

Jade stretches out on the couch and wedges her toes under my thigh. She says, "My feet are cold."

I think, So put some socks on then, and right away I feel bad. I think things like that all the time now. Little stuff bugs me. The way she peels the bread off her sandwich and only eats the insides. The way she won't laugh until someone else does first. Those sticky notes she puts on everything.

I can't chicken out again. It's not fair to either of us.

I slide my tongue across my teeth, then turn and look at her. She's leaning her head against the arm of the couch. Her textbook's propped up in front of her face. All I can see is the top of her ponytail.

It's weird. I haven't been this nervous since the first time I saw her. I sat behind her on the bus looking at that yellow hair for months before I even had the guts to say hi.

When I finally did, it was like pushing a button. I opened my mouth—and Jade started talking as if she'd known me forever. I barely heard a word she said. I just kept thinking, Now what do I do? (I didn't have to worry. She had that figured out too.)

That was a long time ago. I've spent almost all of high school with one girl. A nice, pretty, smart girl—but still, just one girl.

I've got to do this.

"Jade," I say. She keeps reading. My mouth's too dry to talk anyway. I swish some spit around and try again.

"Jade?" She flops the book down flat on her legs and looks at me. She's smiling, but not really. I should know better than to interrupt her when she's studying. It's that kind of smile.

I say, "There's something I need to talk to you about." My voice sounds normal enough. It doesn't crack or anything, so I think for a second this is going to be all right. I'll say what I have to say, and it'll probably be kind of awkward and sad, but then I'll go home and we can both get started on the rest of our lives.

That's not what happens. Jade bolts up straight. Her mouth is still smiling, but her eyes have changed. She's staring at me like she's an owl or something.

She totally throws me. "You're a really…great person," I say. It sounds so lame, like I'm reading a note someone else wrote.

She says, "Are you breaking up with me?"

Two sentences. That's as far as I get, and already she knows.

What am I supposed to say? Yes? I'm not that harsh. I wanted to talk about all the good things first. Ease her into it. Explain how this isn't about her, how we've both changed, stuff like that.

"Are you breaking up with me?" She says it louder this time. She's wearing an old plaid shirt of mine. She pulls it closed at the neck as if I'm some stranger who caught her in her bathrobe.

I go to say something about how much fun we've had together, but I don't get very far. "Are *you* breaking up with me." It's not a question anymore. It's an accusation. She's practically yelling.

"Jade," I say. I want to calm things down, get them back on track. I stand up. I don't know why. A reflex, I guess. After three years, I'm used to going to her when she's upset.

She freaks. "Don't touch me!"

She hurls her Biology book at me. I jump out of the way. It hits the coffee table, and there's this huge clang. Stuff bounces off. A glass breaks.

She's screaming about what a prick I am and what a coward and how I'm so selfish and I'm only doing this because my friends never liked her, and the whole time I'm just standing there with my hands up like I'm under arrest or something.

I'm almost relieved when I see Gavin standing in his bedroom doorway. Jade turns to look. He starts to wail.

He drops his stuffed kangaroo and runs straight to me. He puts his arms around my leg. "Why are you guys fighting? Don't fight. Don't fight." Little kids crying like that will break your heart. They don't hold back. It's the end of the world for them.

Jade grabs the collar of his pajamas and rips him away from me. "Don't, Gavin. Let go! Mick doesn't like us anymore."

The look on his face. That was the worst. How could she say that to him?

I say, "Jade. No! Gavin…"

She slaps my hand away. "That's what you said!"

"I didn't."

"That's what you said."

She won't let me talk.

"You did so. And now you've upset Gavin and he's going to get a migraine and he'll probably throw up and there's school tomorrow and I've got a biology test and I'm going to be up half the night looking after him. So why don't you just get the hell out of here before you screw anything else up?"

Gavin is covering his ears with his hands and sobbing into Jade's side. She's rubbing his back and glaring at me.

I grab my laptop and go.

I don't know what else to do. Maybe I *am* a coward.

Jade's Diary

Chapter Two

February 26

No, it's not. It's three in the morning, so that makes it February 27.

What a night!! I just got Gavin settled down. I should go to bed myself, but there's too much going on in my head. I have to write it out.

It's probably a good thing Gavin had a migraine. (Not for him, of course ☺)

I couldn't get all worked up over my own problems. I had to take care of his. It gave me a chance to cool down. Things look different now.

The truth is, I've known something was up with Mick for a while. There was that poker game he went to with the guys even though we had a movie planned. Then there was that time he got all pissy just because I made the server take my salad back and that other time he "wanted an early night." I had the feeling he wasn't answering all my calls anymore either.

I couldn't figure it out. This wasn't the Mick I knew. We used to spend every waking minute together. We were the perfect couple. Everyone said that. Then, suddenly, he was like, "Sorry, Jade, I'm doing something with Quinn."

"Sorry, Jade, but it's only five dollars. Don't go getting the waitress in trouble just because you asked for dressing on the side."

"Sorry, Jade. I didn't hear my phone."

I thought I'd done something wrong. I racked my brain to figure out what—and tonight I got the answer. I realized it wasn't what I did. It was what I *didn't* do.

I've been so busy lately with homework and work and looking after Gavin and applying to nursing school that I haven't had time for Mick. He's probably worried I don't care anymore, scared he's going to lose me. If he were someone else, he might have tried to talk to me about it, but Mick's not a talker. Instead, he struck back in the only way he knew how—by deliberately provoking me. It's like he's going, "See? I don't need you either."

I understand that now—although the sad thing is he *does* need me. Mick's got two parents, three grandparents, a brother and a sister, but the fact is, he doesn't really have a family. Not the way Mom and Gavin and I do.

We don't have the big house or the big family reunions or the big trips down south every year, but we do talk to each other. We care about each other. At the Staynors' you're lucky if you hear "Dinner's on" or "Don't leave your hockey gear in the hall." That's their idea of a heartfelt conversation. No wonder Mick always wants to hang out in our crappy little apartment instead of at his place.

When I realized that, I was all ready to call him and say how sorry I was for hurting his feelings, but then Gavin threw up and I didn't have the chance. Now I've changed my mind. I *am* sorry—but I realize that even mentioning Mick's feelings would be wounding him again. He's a guy. He doesn't want to look like a wuss.

So I'm just going to let this go. I'll give him a little space. I'll act like we *both* need to chill out. I want him to be able to come back to me when he's ready—and with his dignity intact. Too bad it wasn't intact tonight.

Oops. I didn't mean that. Neither of us behaved as well as we could have, and I know he feels badly for what he did to Gavin. Emotions were running high—and hey, we *all* have our bad days now and again.

Speaking of which, tomorrow's going to be hell. Bio, Chemistry AND Math. Plus I'm cleaning Mrs. Crespo's apartment after school. I've GOT to go to sleep!

Note to Self

1. Iron pink shirt.
2. Talk to Mr. Panjvani about a reference letter.
3. Finish yearbook write-up.

Mick

Chapter Three

Quinn slams into the locker and slides onto the floor. He's supposedly laughing so hard, he can't stand up. I want to kill him.

I poke my head out from behind the pop machine and look down the hall. He goes "Peekaboo!" then chokes on his own hilariousness. He starts wheezing and hacking like he's some eighty-year-old bingo player.

I make sure Jade's gone, then I swear at him and walk over to my locker. I know she saw me.

I shove him out of the way with my foot so I can get my stuff. "You sat on some gum," I say. He jumps up all indignant, like someone put it there on purpose. I'd laugh, but I'm still too pissed off.

A couple of kids walk by and do it for me. Quinn twists his head over his shoulder and starts picking the gum off his butt.

"You know," he says, "when you told me you broke up with Jade, I thought, All right. The man's finally grown a pair. But no such luck. I mean, what is it now—three weeks later? Four? And you're still playing hide-and-seek?"

I get out my World History books. He can talk all he wants. He doesn't know what it's like.

He stretches the gum out into a long gray scuzzy string. It's gone from someone's mouth to the hall floor to Quinn's ass. It grosses me out just looking at it.

He snaps it off. "Either go back to her or get over it," he says, "because, frankly, this is pathetic."

"Yeah," I say. "It is." I look at him rolling the gum in his hands as if that's what we're talking about, then head down the hall without him.

I don't hear a thing Ms. Hamilton says all class. I've got to smarten up. I need a good mark in World History, but my mind's not there today. I keep thinking about Jade. I know breaking up with her was the right thing to do. It's not that. We were too far gone to fix. But that doesn't mean I don't still care about her.

I hate running into her. She looks like hell. She's so skinny and sad. The worst thing, though, is she makes me think of Gavin. I keep picturing his face the last time I saw him. He was sobbing like I'd drowned his dog or something.

But what can I do? I can't go back with Jade to make her little brother happy. I can't go back with her so she won't lose any more weight. I've just got to tough it out. We'll get over it.

The bell rings. Poli-sci is next. The fastest way there is by the east stairs, but that's the way Jade goes to French. I can handle being in English with her. I mean, it's not like I have any choice. But I've got to avoid her the rest of the time. Quinn can laugh all he wants. I know myself. I'll cave if I'm not careful.

I take the west stairs. I skip the last two steps, turn the corner and almost run right into Jade.

We both jump back as if we hit an invisible force field. Jade squeals. I drop my binder. Papers go flying.

She kneels down to get them at the exact same time I do, and we bonk heads.

We both say, "Sorry," then kind of laugh. People are stampeding to class. We're crammed between the wall and a recycling bin. It's really awkward. We're trying to pick everything up before it gets trampled. Our hands keep meeting, but our eyes don't. If you didn't know we'd just broken up, you'd think we'd just started going out.

Shaun Eckler walks by. He says hey to us, then turns and whispers to Carson Ng.

Jade notices too. She flicks her head their way and rolls her eyes. We both know what they're thinking.

We get up. She hugs her book against her chest and says, "Gee, what are you doing way over here?" She makes it sound like a joke.

I try to come up with some excuse, but I've got nothing. I shake my head like, "Who knows?"

She laughs and says, "Personally, I was trying to avoid you. Lot of good it did me."

Now I laugh. It's a relief to get it out in the open. We stand there, shuffling our feet and sort of smiling at each other.

"Well. Nice running into you," I say.

"Run into. Ha. Ha." She looks good with a little life in her face again. "You and your old-man puns."

The hall's full of people. It's probably not the best time to say this, but I do anyway. "Think we could be friends again someday?"

She clicks her tongue. "Of course! Friends would be great."

She reaches out and touches my hand with her finger. She doesn't look at me. "You know…I've had some time to think about this, and it might sound weird, but I'm glad we broke up. Honestly, I don't have time for a relationship now, especially with GooGoo being so sick and everything."

"Gavin's sick?"

"Oh, you know…" She wobbles her head back and forth. "Long story. I'll tell you later."

The bell rings.

"How sick?" I say, but Jade's already backing away from me down the hall.

"Got to go. Sampson deducts points if you're late." She waves her fingers at me, but then stops and kind of pouts. "Look at you. Don't worry, silly! They're probably just migraines," she says. "It's highly unlikely it's a tumor."

Jade's Diary

Chapter Four

March 22

It's been ages since I wrote, and there's so much to say. The big news is I ran into Mick today. (Wearing the blue hoodie I gave him for Xmas! That's no accident.)

He was coming down the west stairs and practically plowed right into me. (Clearly, great minds think alike.)

You should have seen his face! He went pale, then he went pink, then he just kind of gazed at me in this really deep way. I might have had my doubts before, but not anymore. Looks don't lie. Mick still loves me.

Too bad everything's so weird now. There's nowhere for us to go and work this out. It's all so, I don't know, unnatural or something. We can't have a "normal conversation" in English Lit. The entire class is watching our every move. (I really wish we'd been lower profile before. Nobody talks about how Amy Norman and Jordan Mancini's relationship is going.)

Getting together after school doesn't work either. I'm too busy. We'd have to arrange an actual date—and I can tell Mick's not ready to put himself on the line like that yet. (Life would be so much easier without the male ego always getting in the way.)

Then, of course, there's the whole bizarre Quinn Poulos thing. Seriously, he hovers over Mick like he's his grandmother or something. It's almost funny. You'd swear I was some wicked woman plotting to steal the poor boy's virtue. How can we relax with Quinn practically wiretapping everything we say?

I knew bumping into Mick was going to be our only chance to talk.

It was a bit awkward at first, but that's to be expected. You're used to doing things one way for three years, and then suddenly you have to do them a different way? Of course it's going to be uncomfortable. But I made a little joke, and that's all it took. We both started laughing like the good old days.

I love his laugh.

He dropped his stuff, and we both went to pick it up at the same time. Our hands kept touching. It was almost as if we couldn't help ourselves. I know this sounds corny, but it really was kind of magical. There's a powerful connection between us. We both felt it. Who knows what would have happened if Shaun and Carson didn't come by right then? I wouldn't be surprised if Quinn had them spying on us.

Anyway, it kind of ruined the moment, and we were back to being awkward again. He kept rubbing the back of his neck with his palm. That's what he does when he's nervous, and I've always found it so cute. It makes me want to look after him.

I told him Gavin's headaches were back. I could see how worried he was. I knew that would happen. They were like brothers. He'd do anything for him.

I went to the library after school and searched childhood migraines. The doctor told us before that we had to watch what he ate, but I couldn't believe all the foods that can set them off. Chocolate, hot dogs, cheese, yeast, pepperoni—the list went on and on. I printed it out and taped it to the kitchen cupboard when I got home. I'll have to try and figure out which ones make Gavin sick.

When I was at the library, I also went online to look for a dress to wear to the spring dance. I've lost seven pounds, so I want something that's going to show off my waist. I think I found one—long sleeves but low in the back and with a tight skirt. It's kind of a greeny-blue too, so you just KNOW Mick's going to love it. (Brings out the color of my eyes. He always says that.)

If I could do some extra cleaning for Mrs. Crespo, I might be able to afford it next week.

I should turn out the light. Mom's doing back-to-back shifts all week, so I'm going to be busy.

Note to Self

1. Make appointment for highlights.
2. Write treasury report for Enviro-club meeting.
3. Buy groceries. (Take migraine list.)

Mick

Chapter Five

Everybody's grabbing their stuff and booting it out of class. Friday afternoon. It's always like that. I was slow copying down the notes, so I'm the last one to leave. Ms. Hamilton spots me going out the door and waves me over.

The new girl is standing beside her, so I've got a pretty good idea what this is about. The history test. *Please don't tell me I did as badly as some kid who barely speaks English.*

"Relax, Mick. I'm not going to bite you." Ms. Hamilton doesn't look up. She's writing something in her agenda. "The school board frowns on that sort of thing."

She slaps down her pen and pushes the book aside. "I have a little favor to ask. You know Dalma?"

I say yes, but I don't really, not unless knowing her name counts. She only started here a few days ago.

"Excellent! I just got a text from my son's babysitter. He's been in some sort of…altercation." She pretends to growl. I'm not sure if she's mad at the kid or the babysitter, or if she's even really mad at all.

"I've got to run. Would you mind taking Dalma to the language lab for me? She's supposed to meet her tutor there at three forty-five."

"Sure. No problem." Maybe I didn't do as bad on the test as I thought.

Ms. Hamilton is already shoving her stuff into her briefcase. I'm not sure Dalma is following what's going on. She looks like she's still a little worried about the teacher biting me. Ms. Hamilton nods at her and smiles. "That okay with you?"

Before Dalma can answer, Ms. Hamilton has switched off the lights and hustled us out the door. "Thanks, Mick," she says. "You're a peach!"

She's halfway down the hall when she turns around. "Oh, sorry. Better tell her what that means, Mick."

Then she's gone. I can hear her high heels clacking down the hall. She really picks up speed when she gets out of sight. Something about that seems funny to me. I sort of chuckle. Dalma does too, although I don't know if we're laughing at the same thing.

"This way," I say and point toward the east stairs. It feels really formal, like I'm showing her to her seat in a fancy restaurant. She nods. We start walking.

We're quiet for a while, and then Dalma says, "Peach?" It takes me a second to understand what she's talking about. She brings her hand in front of her mouth as if she's holding a ball and pretends to take a bite.

"Oh, right," I say. "Yeah. That's it. Peach."

"*You* are peach?" She laughs. A big loud "ha!" It surprises me. I laugh at her laugh, then try to cover it up by sounding like I'm laughing at her joke. I say, "No, that's not what it means exactly."

She wipes her hand across her forehead like she's going, "Phew!" Her eyes are so brown, they're practically black. The hall lights leave little white squares in them.

"So what it mean exactly?"

I rub the back of my neck and try to explain. "It means I'm, like, a good guy."

"You are?"

"Well, that's what it means. I don't know if I am or not."

She pretends to be shocked.

"You don't know you are a good guy? You are maybe bad guy?"

My face is hot. "No, no. I'm good."

"Therefore I am safe with you?"

I laugh. "Yes, you are safe with me."

I'm just realizing she's kind of pretty when I see Jade coming out of Mr. Panjvani's class. I jerk like someone snapped me with an elastic band.

Dalma notices. "Something is not good?" she says.

"No, no. It's nothing." It's been over a month since we broke up. Jade said she didn't want a relationship. I can talk to another girl if I want.

"Mick, hey!" Jade scurries over. I don't know what to do with my face. She kisses my cheek.

My forehead suddenly feels really itchy. Dalma looks back and forth between the two of us. Jade clicks her fingernails on her binder.

"Um. This is Dalma. She's new. I'm just taking her to the language lab." I sound guilty. I didn't need to say where we're going.

"Oh, hi, I'm Jade!" Big smile, handshake. She seems okay. "New? From where?"

"My country?"

"Yes."

"Croatia."

"Wow! Long way. I hear it's beautiful."

"Yes. Very beautiful."

Jade asks about her family and how well Dalma knows the city and if she likes school and if she's having any trouble getting around or finding places to shop. Jade should speak a little slower.

The clock in the hall reads 3:42.

"Ah, we better get going," I say. "The tutor's waiting."

"Can I take her?" Jade asks. "I'm going right past the lab anyway, and it'd give me a chance to tell her about the Newcomers Club."

I shrug. It's not my decision.

Jade smiles at Dalma to see if it's okay with her.

Dalma looks at me.

Jade says, "He won't mind!" She takes Dalma's arm and starts walking away. "You heard about the Newcomers Club? Every second Thursday in the multipurpose room, three-thirty to five. We're here to make arriving students feel welcome."

Jade seems to remember me at the last minute. "Oh, sorry. Bye, Mick!"

She blows me a kiss. Dalma makes this goofy face, like "What's going on here?" I shrug again. I don't know.

On the way home, I realize I didn't ask about Gavin. I figure he must be doing okay. Jade seemed happy.

Jade's Diary

Chapter Six

March 30

I shouldn't say this, but it was almost funny running into Mick today. He's so transparent. He shows up outside Mr. Panjvani's room with another girl, then tries to act all surprised to see me there.

Hello-o. I've been taking that class all year. I always stay late on Fridays to help put the equipment away. He knows that better than anyone. Of course I'm going to be there!

I wonder what he was expecting. Some kind of jealous rage? Me running off in tears? He's really not very good at this kind of thing—but that's one of the many reasons I love him. He's not phony. Mick can't act a certain way if he's not that way.

Can you imagine if it were Quinn trying to make me jealous? He'd have had the whole thing worked out. He'd have picked the hottest girl in school, and they'd be deep in the throes of passion right when I walked out the door.

Mick, on the other hand, looked like he was eight years old and his teacher had made him stand next to a girl in the bus lineup. You've got to wonder what poor Dalma was thinking. It couldn't have been very comfortable for her either. They barely looked at each other.

Honestly, I felt obliged to put them out of their misery. That's the only reason I offered to walk her to the language lab.

Her English isn't very good, but she's actually kind of sweet. I told her about Newcomers and left my number with the tutor in case he wanted me to give her some extra help during the week. She doesn't have a phone yet, which is too bad. I think she and Kevin Peters might hit it off. He's been wanting a girlfriend for ages, and he does like the tall ones! She'd be perfect.

Maybe we could double-date sometime. Her and Kevin, me and Mick. Wouldn't that be ironic?

On another topic entirely...I'm a little annoyed at Mick. Not about the Dalma thing. (That's almost touching, when you think about it. I mean, he wouldn't have gone to all that trouble if he didn't care!) It's about Gavin.

Mick asked me a couple of times in English class how he was doing, but since then—nothing. I expected him to be more concerned that that. He didn't even *mention* Gavin today.

I hope he hasn't forgotten about him. I wouldn't want that to happen.

Note to Self

1. Set up meeting for Dalma with Newcomers Club.
2. Talk to Kevin P.
3. Send in application for nursing school.

Mick

Chapter Seven

Jade's not in English class today.
It shouldn't make any difference, but
it does. I stretch my legs out under her
chair and let myself get comfortable.
I haven't done that since we broke up.

"Jade...Jade Nelson?" Mr. Ubu
looks up from his attendance sheet.
"Does anyone know where Jade is?"

Lily Crouse says, "She just texted me. She was in a car accident."

I sit up straight. Everyone turns around and starts talking. It's an excuse as much as anything, and Ubu knows it.

"Class. Class!" He presses his hands down in front of him like he's demonstrating how to do a push-up.

"Jade is still capable of tapping out a detailed message. Clearly, this was not a catastrophic accident. Now settle down. And Lily, put your phone away. You know the rules."

He starts writing on the board. I lean over to Lily. "What happened?"

She shakes her head. "I think it's Gavin. She said she has to take him to the hospital."

That's all I get before Ubu claps chalk dust off his hands and faces the class again.

He's wrong. Just because Jade can still text doesn't mean she's okay. I know her. She could be gushing blood from her brain, and she'd still make sure she didn't have an "unexplained absence" on her record. She's dying to get into nursing school.

Dying.

I warned her mother about that crap car of theirs. I can't believe it ever passed inspection. The muffler's held on with duct tape, and I'm not even exaggerating. I walked home in the freezing rain one night rather than get in that death trap.

Mr. Ubu says, "Turn to chapter four."

Gavin is four.

I should have called. I should have gone around and seen him, taken him to the playground or out for an ice cream or something.

What does Jade mean by an accident? How bad of an accident?

My eyes sting. It would be so lame if I started to cry.

I tell myself Quinn's right. I had to walk away from them. I couldn't be going back to their place all the time. Gavin already went through that once when his dad left. I couldn't let him get his hopes up again. It's like that thing they say about pulling off a Band-Aid. Do it fast. It'll hurt less in the long run.

That's what I tell myself, but as soon as class ends, I'm out of there like a shot.

I try Jade's cell phone. She doesn't pick up. No answer at her mother's either. I'd call Gavin's preschool, but I don't remember the name.

The bell rings for second period. Math. It's midterm review today. I can't miss it. I'll try Jade again later.

I head straight to class. If I hadn't had to walk by the door to the parking lot, I bet I would have made it. Instead, I grab

Anwar and ask him to tell Mr. Lawson I have to go to the hospital. At least I'm not lying about that.

Luckily, it's my day for the car. I gun it to the children's hospital. The whole way there, I'm hunched over the wheel with these pictures flashing in my mind. It's like I'm watching the lead-in to the five o'clock news. A paramedic pulling a little kid's body out of a smashed car. Heart-wrenching close-up of a stuffed kangaroo by the wreck. The reporter shaking her head and doing her best sad face. "The name of the victim cannot be identified until next of kin have been notified. And now over to you, Ted."

I park with one wheel up on the curb and run through the hospital's emergency entrance. The waiting room is half empty. I look around. I don't see them.

That's either a good sign or a very bad one.

The security guard says, "Yes?" I turn and stare at him. I'm trying to come up with a way to ask the question I want to ask without making an idiot of myself.

"Can I help you?" he says.

At that exact moment, the sliding door opens and there's Gavin. A nurse is pushing him in a wheelchair. His arm is wrapped in a big bandage. Angie, his mother, is right behind him. She's holding Kanga. That seems kind of funny to me. The kangaroo survived too. I almost laugh.

"Mick," she says. Jade looks up from her cell phone. Gavin jumps out of the wheelchair and runs right at me.

"Careful!" I say. I don't want to hurt him.

The nurse says, "A remarkable recovery."

Angie laughs, then nods at me. "You can pick him up. Don't worry."

She points at the bandage and whispers, "It's mostly for show. Although heaven knows I wish I'd listened to you about that damn car."

She puts her hand on her throat and manages not to cry. She's a nice lady. I feel bad for her. Since her husband left, all she does is work.

I hoist Gavin up, and he throws his arms around my head. I can barely see. He's sticky. He smells like grape juice and pee. I really really missed him.

"Mick," Jade says. I move Gavin's wrist from my eyes and look at her. I almost forgot she was here. "You're so sweet to come," she says.

"You okay?"

"Oh. Yeah. Fine." She waves a hand. "More worried about you-know-who than anything."

Gavin says, "Who?"

We all say, "Nobody."

Angie's on a double shift at the adult hospital, so I take the others home. It's like having a chimp in the car. If Gavin weren't strapped into his car seat, he'd be banging his head on the ceiling.

He's babbling away about preschool and the crash and the cop and the nurse. Everything is, "Know what, Mick?" or "Guess what, Mick," or "That's the truth, Mick." He must have used my name thirty times.

Jade leans against the passenger door and wiggles her eyebrows. "Someone's happy to see you."

"The feeling's mutual," I say. "I'm so glad he's okay. I mean, so glad you're both okay."

"We are now," Jade says.

We pull into the building's parking lot. Jade gets Gavin out of his car seat. She flinches when she picks him up.

"Here," I say. "I'll carry him." I kind of forgot she was in the accident too.

They live on the fourth floor and, as usual, the elevator's not working. I'm huffing by the time we get to the top of the stairs.

"Can you come in for a while?" Jade says.

Gavin bounces up and down in my arms. "Yes, yes, yes!"

No getting out of it. "Just for a minute," I say.

Jade opens the door. I've always liked the smell of their place. She and Angie drink a lot of ginger tea. There's something about it that seems kind of Christmasy or something. Today, though, it just seems sad. It's like it was going into going into Nanny's house after the funeral and smelling her perfume.

Gavin drags me into the kitchen. He wants a snack. "Just be careful what you give him," Jade says. "There's a list of stuff he can't have on the cupboard door."

"Okay, bud, what'll it be?" I plop Gavin onto the counter and look at the list. It's, like, a page long. I don't have time for this.

Chocolate. Coffee. Aged cheese.

"What's sodium nitrate?" I say.

Jade's in the living room, putting Gavin's jacket and shoes away. "Something in hot dogs and salami."

Artificial sweeteners. Chicken livers.

As if a preschooler's going to want chicken livers for a snack.

"MSG?" I say.

"It's a spice or something. Sort of looks like salt. They put it in Chinese food."

No Chinese food. Now that hurts.

"Sulphites?"

"You don't have to worry about them. They're in red wine."

I point my finger at Gavin and say, "Keep out of the red wine, buddy." He rolls his eyes so he looks drunk. Or, at least, so he looks the way a four-year-old thinks someone looks when they're drunk. He cracks me up.

I call out to Jade, "So what can he have, then?"

"How about a peanut-butter-and-jam sandwich?"

She couldn't just tell me that in the first place? I remember why she used to irritate me.

I get out a couple slices of bread, smear one side with peanut butter and load the other side up with jam. Just the way he likes it. We have a little snicker over that. Gavin loves thinking he's getting away with something.

I put the sandwich on his Batman plate and cut it into four triangles. He sits on the counter, eating and talking, while I put everything away.

They might not have much money, but Jade and Angie are neat freaks.

"Okay, bud," I say. "Got to go."

Jade is leaning against the kitchen doorway, smiling at me. I hope she didn't see how much jam I gave him. She's changed into that old plaid shirt of mine.

"You do?"

"Yeah," I say. "I've got History starting soon. I have to run."

Gavin starts to whine, but Jade stops him. "Now, now, GooGoo. Mick's right. School's important," she says.

She kisses me on the cheek. I ruffle Gavin's hair, then race off to class. I really don't want to miss it. Dalma's going to be there.

Jade's Diary

Chapter Eight

April 2

The big accident! Or, should I say, the big, HAPPY accident.

The policeman was so sweet. I told him a cat darted in front of the car, and he was totally sympathetic. Said it could happen to anyone. He made me promise, though, that next time I wouldn't risk my life to save anything "that low on the food chain." (I think he kind of liked me.)

He doesn't have to worry. Trust me. I'd never do that again. IT WAS SCARY!!!!! I thought I was just going to slide off into the ditch, but then we hit that boulder and almost rolled. I was shaking so hard when I texted Lily. I must have made a million typos.

Constable Cheng looked us over and said he didn't think we needed to go to the hospital, but I made him take us anyway. Not for my sake. For Gavin's. He's such a brave little guy because of all the pain he's endured. Sometimes it's hard to know when he's actually hurt.

My eyes filled up with tears when I said that. I guess I've been under more stress than I realized these last six weeks—but whatever. It worked. Constable Cheng took us straight there.

He insisted on calling Mom even though I begged him not to. I said I didn't want her to worry and that we needed the money. No one's going to pay her for sitting around in the emergency room. But he wouldn't listen. He said it would make me feel better.

What *actually* made me feel better was Mick. I was surprised—but not really—to see him come barreling into the ER. It's when bad things happen that people show their true colors.

Then when I saw him hug Gavin? I can't even think about that without getting misty-eyed again. It was so sweet and so genuine. I felt surrounded by love.

The funny thing is, I really do mean it when I say I'm happy we broke up. We'd gotten used to each other. I almost couldn't see him anymore. Now he walks into a room, and my heart goes crazy. I forgot how beautiful his eyes are.

Those little specks of green. How could I have forgotten about them?

And I love how tall he is. Most big guys stand with their heads up and their shoulders way back. They flaunt it. But Mick kind of bends down to your level. You don't feel like you're small or he's doing you a favor. You just feel kind of looked after.

I didn't appreciate that before, but I do now. It's time we got back to normal.

Note to Self

1. Call garage about car.
2. Take early lunch.

Mick

Chapter Nine

Quinn is mooching French fries off my plate again.

"Get your own." I jab at his hand with my fork.

"Now, now," he says. "That's no way to impress the ladies." He lifts his chin in the direction of the salad bar. I turn and see Dalma coming toward us with a tray full of food. He steals half my fries while I'm looking at her, but I don't really care anymore.

"I can sit?" she says. Her hair is so smooth and shiny, it's like metal. Liquid metal, if there is such a thing.

Quinn goes, "Here, take my place" and gets up. "I was leaving anyway." He's the type of guy who thinks he sounds smooth even with his mouth full.

Dalma asks him to stay, but he shakes his head. He swipes his elbow across the table and brushes the grunge he left onto the floor. "For you, Lady Dalma." He bows at her, then gives me a big sleazy wink, tongue out the side of his mouth and everything. "Later, Mick."

She puts down her tray, tucks her hair behind her ear and watches him go. She's wearing little gold hoops. "How he knows my name?"

Because I'm an idiot and told him about you even though I know he's got a big mouth. I don't say that.

I move a chicken nugget around my plate with my fork. "Everyone knows you. You're the new girl."

"Ah!" She bats her eyelashes. "I am starlet?"

That makes me laugh. Where would Dalma pick up a word like *starlet*? It's something my great-aunt would say.

"Would you like to go to a movie with me tonight?" I don't know where that came from, either.

She pulls back, eyes wide. "Me?"

"Yes."

"And you?"

"Yes."

"To movie?"

"Yes."

"Okay," she says, then laughs. She takes a big bite of salad. Her whole face keeps smiling, even while she chews. She doesn't seem afraid of anything.

Some dressing dribbles down her chin.

I point at it. She looks behind her, then shrugs. "I see nothing."

"I mean, your chin," I say.

She squints one eye at me suspiciously. "How I can see my chin?"

This doesn't need to be so complicated.

I take my napkin, reach across the table and wipe the dressing off her face. In the process, I leave behind a smear of honey-garlic dipping sauce. I probably should have used a clean napkin.

For some reason, this strikes me as hilarious. I cover my mouth and laugh really hard.

Dalma goes, "What? What?"

She's laughing too, but still, I shouldn't leave her like that. I pound on my chest until I can pull myself together, then pick up an unused napkin, dip it in my water and try again. She scrunches up her face the way Gavin would if I was doing it to him.

"My mother. She do this." Dalma pretends to spit into her hand, then rubs it back and forth in the air.

"Same here." We both go, "Ew."

"Look," Dalma says. "Your friend."

She waves. I turn and see Jade coming toward us. She usually has late lunch on Thursdays. I lift my hand. It's not quite a wave.

"Chicken nuggets." Jade nudges me with her elbow, then slides into the chair next to me. "I should have known." She looks at Dalma. "He can't resist them."

I don't think Dalma knows the word *resist*, but she smiles anyway.

Jade peels open her tub of no-fat yogurt. She scrapes tiny little blobs off the foil lid, then puts the spoon upside down on her tongue. It's not the most efficient way to eat. The whole time, she's talking to Dalma about the Newcomers Club, her tutor, the dress she's wearing to the spring dance and Kevin Peters. I have no idea why she's talking about Kevin. I didn't even think she knew him that well. I'm positive Dalma doesn't know him at all. I nod and say stuff like "Oh yeah?" and "No kidding," but basically I'm out of the conversation.

The bell goes. We take our trays and dump the leftovers in the bins on the way out. Jade's only eaten about two tablespoons of yogurt.

"Shouldn't you finish that?" I say. "You'll get hungry." By which I mean "even skinnier." It's none of my business, but I'm seriously considering calling her mother about how much weight she's lost. I wonder if she's anorexic.

Jade looks at Dalma. "He always worries about me. It's so cute." She gives my arm a little slap.

We head down the hall. It's really noisy. People are slamming lockers shut, bombing between classes, screaming at each other about stuff. Rory Steinberg jumps off the landing and practically knocks Kyle Dodds over. That's not as funny as he thinks it's going to be.

It must be hard for Dalma to understand what Jade's saying with all the racket. I'll have to find a quiet place to ask her about tonight. I don't know where she lives yet.

Jade turns to go. "Oh, hey, Dalma. I'm thinking of having some girls over for pizza tonight. Why don't you come?"

Dalma slumps her head to one side. "Sorry. I cannot. I go…" She points her hand at me. "I mean, we go…" she says. I don't know if it's the look on my face or the look on Jade's, but Dalma stops talking.

"Oh, too bad," Jade says. "Next time!" She twiddles her fingers at us, then runs up the stairs to Chemistry.

I arrange to pick Dalma up at her place at seven.

Jade's Diary

Chapter Ten

April 15

I learned a few things today.

The first is that MSG *definitely* brings on Gavin's migraines. He had a little tiny bit tonight and boom. Just like that, he was crying and screaming and throwing up. The whole nine yards. It was ugly.

The second thing I learned is that I can count on Mick. I don't know why I keep doubting it. I called him tonight when I realized how bad this was going to be. I was really apologetic about it. I knew he was doing something with Dalma, and she can't have many friends yet, so it was probably disappointing for her too—but what choice did I have? Mom can't be leaving work every time Gavin's sick.

I didn't have to explain that to Mick. He understands. He immediately went, "Don't worry. I'll be right there."

Twenty minutes later, he was at the door. Poor Dalma. I wonder if she had to take the bus home.

The two of us managed to get Gavin cleaned up and settled down. Then Mick put him to bed. It was so adorable. Light really bothers Gavin's eyes when he's having a migraine, so Mick couldn't turn on the lamp to read him a story. Not that he needed to. Mick's put him to bed enough times that he knows the words by heart. The two of them lay in the pitch-dark, flipping pages, while Mick "read" *Go Dog Go*. So sweet.

Then he made me some toast and positively slathered it with peanut butter. He didn't seem to care about how fat that was going to make me. We snuggled on the couch and, for a while, it was just like it used to be.

That's when I learned the third thing. I can't rush him. I don't want to scare him away.

Note to Self

1. Only fruit and water tomorrow.
2. And be patient!

Mick

Chapter Eleven

Quinn drags his hand down his face. "You're not serious."

I start stuffing my gear into my duffel bag. I should never have mentioned it.

"She called you when you were already at the movie with Dalma—and you actually left?" He wipes the ice off his blades and laughs.

"Jade's playing you," he says.

I'm meeting Dalma in a few minutes by the flagpole. I don't want to talk about this now.

"Seriously. She's playing you," he says again.

I give my duffel bag a shove. "How?" I say. "Come on. Tell me. How?"

Quinn looks at the ceiling like he can't believe he has to spell this out for me. "It's so obvious. She sees you with someone else, and immediately she's got some big crisis only you can solve."

"Her little brother had a migraine," I say.

"And you're the only one who can help? Where's her mother?"

"Working."

"Her father?"

"Who knows?"

"What about a relative…a neighbor… nine-one-one?"

I grab my shoulder pads and ram them into my duffel bag.

"I should have said to Jade, 'Call nine-one-one. I'm going to a movie.' That's what you're telling me?"

Quinn stands up and zips his fly. "Yeah. Sorta. She's not your problem anymore." He sniffs his T-shirt. Even from here I can tell it's rank, but he puts it on anyway.

"She's pulling your chain, Mick. Trust me. You keep responding to her, she'll keep making crap up."

I've got my helmet in my hand. I consider slamming it into his head but put it away instead. "She didn't make anything up," I say. "I was there. I saw Gavin. He had a migraine."

"Maybe he's in on it too." Quinn leans over the sink to check his so-called sideburns in the mirror.

"He's four years old. You think a four-year-old can make himself throw up? Go pale? He's a preschooler, Quinn, not Ryan frigging Gosling."

"Fine. Whatever." He turns and looks right at me. "But you don't think this is a little strange? You're out on your first date in—what?—three years, and suddenly Jade absolutely needs you to drop everything and rush right over?"

I close up my duffel bag. There's no point arguing with him.

"What can I tell you, Quinn? Coincidences happen. If she needs help with Gavin, she needs help with Gavin. I'm not going to desert her." I grab my jacket. "I gotta go. Dalma's waiting."

"That's what I'm talking about. How long you think she's going to wait while you're off looking after your ex-girlfriend's little brother? You're not the only guy around here interested in her."

I push open the change-room door. "Thanks for that, Quinn."

"Dude. Just trying to be your friend."

I walk through the rink. I wave across the ice at the coach. Jade has always said Quinn didn't like her. Maybe she's right.

Then I think about last night, and I wonder.

No question about it. Gavin was really sick when I got there. He must have puked five times. Jade might have been able to handle it herself, but she was worn out. I could see that. Anyone could see that. Dalma and I could go to a movie another time.

I lay in the dark with Gavin until he fell asleep. I checked my phone. It wasn't that late. Dalma had said I could drop by any time before eleven.

When I came out of the bedroom, Jade was sitting on the couch, folding laundry. Her Chemistry book was open on her lap. I felt sorry for her.

I'd never felt sorry for her before. I'd just figured that's the way she is. The perfect little A student. But then I saw her there on a Friday night, cleaning up, studying, taking care of Gavin—doing all the stuff she has to do just to survive—and I thought, Frig. No wonder she called me.

"GooGoo asleep?" she said.

I nodded.

"Good. Give me a minute, I'll be done here soon too."

I sat down on the couch next to her. She can't do this alone anymore, I thought. She needs help. Problem is, who's going to help? Her mother's working. Her dad's a deadbeat. Gavin's dad is too. They can't afford to pay anyone. Even the doctors don't do much good. Jade says they just tell her to be careful about what he eats, make sure he gets enough sleep and give him a headache pill as soon as the migraine starts—it'll only last a few hours. Lot of help that is. Someone still has to look after him. I don't see any solution.

I closed her textbook and put it on the coffee table. One thing she didn't need to be doing was studying on a Friday night. That much I knew. I started folding towels. It was the only thing I could think to do for her.

She went "Aw…" and patted my arm.

She shifted a little closer to me. I didn't think much about it. She might have just been getting comfortable. Then she pulled her legs up onto the couch. Then she leaned her head on my shoulder.

I could see where that was going. I panicked. I did this really lame, "Oh, would you look at the time?" thing and took off as fast as I could.

Quinn's wrong about Jade. She didn't make the problem up. But I get the feeling she wouldn't mind taking advantage of it.

Dalma is waiting for me by the flag-pole outside the rink. She's shivering.

She's not used to what we call spring around here. I open up my jacket and wrap her in it.

"Where do you want to go?"

"Surprise me," she says.

Jade's Diary

Chapter Twelve

April 18

I feel sorry for Dalma. She's just moved to a new country. She barely speaks the language. She's vulnerable. Mick should be careful not to lead her on. She could easily mistake his kindness for something else.

I saw that today. I had a spare period. Everyone was hanging out by the back door. I went over to say hi to Mick, and my phone rang. Two o'clock on the nose. Gavin's preschool. He was having another migraine. When I mentioned our car was still in the garage, Mick didn't hesitate. Not even for a second. He said, "I'll take you."

Dalma said, "I hope your little brother is okay"—or at least something more or less like that—but she had this strange look on her face, as if she was surprised Mick would just up and go. It made me wonder if he's told her about us.

I was trying not to cry, so we didn't talk much on the drive over to the daycare. The only thing I really remember is Mick putting his hand on mine and saying, "Don't worry. It'll be fine." And of course once he said that, it was.

When we got to Tiny Tykes, Shirley was sitting with Gavin in the rocking chair. He was white as a ghost. Mick covered his eyes from the sunlight and brought him to the car. He put him in his car seat, told him to hug Kanga, then drove really slowly to the apartment. I didn't need to tell him a thing. It's like we have one brain. He knows exactly what to do.

Gavin vomited when we got upstairs. Mick cleaned it up while I gave Gavin a bath. He was feeling a little better by then, so I left them together and went off to pick up a frozen mac and cheese for our lunch. When I came back, the two of them were sound asleep on the couch.

I don't want to have babies yet. I really don't. I want to get my nursing degree and start my career, but...but... seeing Mick lying there with Gavin in his arms, I couldn't help thinking what a great dad he would make. Especially if the kids got his eyes.

And his hands.

And that funny smile of his.

(I'm bad...)

Note to Self

1. Arrange for babysitter for spring dance.

2. Decide about long hair or updo.

Mick

Chapter Thirteen

We're in my car in front of her place. I've turned off the engine. I lean over to kiss her, but I can tell something's wrong. I sit back and look at her.

"Dalma?" I say.

"Yes?" Even *yes* is funny when she says it.

Her arms are folded on her lap. It's not the most inviting pose.

"Why you smile?" she says.

"I like you."

She turns and looks out the windshield, as if there's something to see other than some garbage bags out for tomorrow's pickup.

"No," she says. "I think you like Jade." She pronounces it "Yade."

I shake my head. I say, "No, no, no, no, no."

I reach over and take her hand. "I know that's what this looks like, but that's wrong. It's just Gavin. Her little brother. He's sick. She needs my help. That's all this is."

I yammer on for a while. Dalma's hand has gone kind of limp in mine. She doesn't believe me. I tell her how long Jade and I went out, how we're still friends, how I'm really close to Gavin— but that only makes it worse.

"Dalma, please," I say.

I sit there, holding her hand, looking at her. After a while, she turns and looks at me too. I get the feeling that if I can say the right thing, it'll be okay.

Her father's strict. I've got ten minutes to make my case, then she has to be inside.

I think of Gavin, puking on the kitchen floor. I think of Jade and her pile of laundry and her lunches to make and her homework to do. I think of Quinn saying I'm not the only guy interested in Dalma.

I rub her fingers. They're long and straight—I wasn't surprised at all when she told me she plays the piano. I really like her.

"Dalma, I promise. This isn't going to happen again. I'm going to take care of this."

Jade's Diary

Chapter Fourteen

April 24

It's as if Mick has just disappeared. He isn't in the cafeteria at lunchtime anymore. He wasn't shooting hoops in his third-period spare. On Tuesday, he wasn't even in English class. He was there Wednesday, but he barely said hi.

It is starting to worry me. We've come so far in the last couple of weeks—then this. I don't know if I can stand the emotional roller coaster anymore. (Especially since my dress arrived yesterday for the spring dance. I'm not even sure we're going yet!)

I got Gavin to sleep, then I had a little cry. This doesn't make any sense. Why is Mick acting this way? We were so much happier when we were together. If he'd just relax and spend some time with me again, he'd see that. He's got to stop listening to Quinn. He's got to stop whatever he thinks he's doing with Dalma. He can't keep screwing up our lives this way.

I felt so sad and mad and frustrated. I tried to do some ironing, but I had to stop. I was afraid I'd burn something.

I stood there for the longest time, staring at the steam coming out of the iron. I burned myself before. I remember how much it hurt. It was right before Dad left. He put this special ointment on it and let me stay up late watching TV with him. I was only seven, but the scar's still there.

That made me cry again, and I don't have time for that. I said, "Jade. Pull yourself together. You're being ridiculous. You're a strong person. You're a good person. You work hard. You deserve to be happy. It will hurt for a while, but you can do it."

I wiped the tears away, and then I got up. I put my books away and decided what I was going to wear tomorrow. I made Gavin his lunch. I gave him a little extra this time, just to be on the safe side.

Now I've just got to figure out which shoes to get for the dance. I'm worried the teal ones might be too old-ladyish. I've got to make up my mind by tomorrow, or they won't be here in time for the dance.

Note to Self
1. Text Lily BEFORE English class.
2. Check Mom's work schedule.

Mick

Chapter Fifteen

I've been driving Dalma to school almost every day. It's going to get me in trouble. I can't seem to make it from the parking lot to class on time.

I walk into English with a big smile on my face. Ubu goes, "Why, if it isn't the late great Mr. Staynor." I brace myself, but all he says is, "How wonderful to see someone so obviously delighted to take my class."

Jade's been late a few times herself, so I don't notice her empty seat until he calls her name for attendance. I'm flipping through my textbook, trying to remember if there was anything I was supposed to do for today, when Lily says, "She quit."

Mr. Ubu takes off his glasses. They dangle by the string around his neck. "Quit?" He's as shocked as I am.

Lily checks her phone. "That's what she said."

"Quit English?" Ubu loves Jade. She's his star student.

"No. Quit school."

The whole class starts to talk. I hear someone mention my name, and Fariq say something about Jade's little brother, but mostly I zone out. This is bad news. I can feel it.

Ubu rubs his hand back and forth over his head a few times, then says, "All right. Enough. Turn to page two hundred and sixty-nine. Let's hear what our friend Bill Shakespeare has to say about the vicissitudes of life."

He asks me what *vicissitude* means. He's told us before, but I say I don't know. He lets me off. He asks Kyle instead. He must know I'm upset.

I call Jade as soon as class is out, but there's no answer. No answer after Chemistry or Biology either.

I've been here before. Part of me thinks she's not picking up the phone because she wants me to worry.

The other part of me thinks she's in the hospital with Gavin. I've googled migraines before. All the pages say the same thing. They're painful but not serious. Kids get them all the time. Most grow out of them. Gavin's got all the classic symptoms. There's no reason to worry.

Then I remember Jade saying, "It's probably not a tumor." I'm standing in the school lobby, staring at the trophy case, and it hits me. *Probably not* means almost exactly the same thing as *might be.*

I promised Dalma I wasn't going to let this happen again, so I meet her for lunch like we planned. I don't say a thing about Jade. Afterward, I walk her to class. She reminds me about dinner tonight at her place.

"I can hardly wait," I say.

She says, "Sure," and we both laugh. We had a long talk yesterday about how sometimes *sure* means the opposite of what it sounds like.

"No, really," I say. "I love intestines."

We laugh some more. She told me they eat cow intestines in Croatia.

I'm not sure if she was joking. Her English is really improving, but we still have some misunderstandings. I hope this is one of them.

I'd kiss her goodbye, but Ms. Lumsden says, "So long, loverboy" and pulls the door closed.

I go out into the parking lot and try Jade again. She's still not answering. I think of calling Angie, but I don't want to make things worse. This could just be one of Jade's moods, and I can talk her out of it.

I get into the car and drive to her apartment. I'm not doing this for her or even Gavin anymore. I'm doing this for me. I'm never going to be able to get on with my own life until this problem is solved. I think Jade should talk to the guidance counselor. Mr. Brownell's a nice guy. He'll know what to do.

I run upstairs. Someone's home. I can hear movement. I knock. The sound stops. I knock again. Nothing.

"Jade? It's me."

It goes even quieter. I can actually hear the silence inside.

"Jade?"

Footsteps, then the door opens a crack. "I'm busy, Mick." She's whispering.

"Just for a second? Jade. Please. We need to talk. I won't stay long."

She lets the door creak open but turns her back and walks away before I get a look at her.

The place is a mess. Toys everywhere. Unfolded laundry. What looks like last night's dinner. I don't see any barf, but I can smell it.

Jade sits down on the couch. She's wearing baggy sweatpants and that old shirt of mine. She's obviously been crying.

The skin around her eyes is all pink and blotchy.

"You okay?"

She nods and starts throwing Gavin's toys into a rubber bin. She won't look at me. I move some laundry aside and sit next to her on the couch.

"Jade. You can't quit school."

She rubs her fingers up and down her forehead.

"Jade. You can't. This is crazy." I touch her back. I can feel her shaking. "There's a way around this. There has to be."

She swings around. She's whispering, but her voice is as hard as if she were screaming.

"How? GooGoo's sick. I take him to the doctor's. I take him to the hospital. No one can help him. Certainly not his parents…"

"What about talking to Mr. Brownell?"

"You think I haven't?" Her chin is trembling. She puts her hand over her mouth.

My parents would help. I know they would, but I'm afraid to say that to Jade, not when she's like this. She's never liked them very much, and she's proud, too. I'm not sure she'd want that.

"You're exhausted," I say. "You should go to bed. Get some sleep. I'll stay here." She closes her eyes. Tears pour down her face. I put my arm around her and help her up. I'll talk to Mom about it later.

"Why don't you sleep in your mother's room? It's nice and quiet there." Jade normally sleeps on the couch. She's so tiny and frail, I almost want to carry her. She doesn't put up any fuss.

"Why is Jadie crying?"

Gavin is hugging Kanga and peering at me from behind his door. Jade turns into my side so he can't see her face.

"Just tired, buddy," I say. "I'm going to put her to bed, then you and I are going to the park."

He starts running on the spot and waving his hands. His headache must be better.

I tell him to get ready, then help Jade into bed. I grab a box of Kleenex from the chest of drawers and put it on the nightstand. She takes my hand and pulls me down closer to her. "Thank you, Mick. You know I couldn't do this without you." She goes to say something else but starts to cry again.

"Don't worry, Jade," I say. "We'll figure this out. I promise."

I turn out the light and close the door. Gavin is already dressed and raring to go.

Jade's Diary

Chapter Sixteen

April 25

Why does he do this to me? I should never have opened the door. I shouldn't have let him in.

He acts like he cares so much. Like he's a good guy. He touches my arm. He holds me. He looks me in the eye and he's all like, "Jade. Please."

"Let me help."

"Don't worry."

Or my favorite: "We'll figure this out."

We'll—like we're a couple. Like we're in this together.

And I believe him! I'm finally feeling okay, like this nightmare has finally ended. I get up from my nap. Have a shower. Wash my hair. Clean the living room. Get dinner ready—home-made spaghetti, just the way he likes it.

He walks in the door carrying Gavin. They both have rosy cheeks and smell of outside. He says, "I bought Gavin a banana. I hope that's okay. I checked the migraine list before I left, and I didn't think it was one of the triggers."

"No, no," I say. "That's fine. I just hope it doesn't ruin his appetite. You guys must be starved."

He looks at me, and he looks at the table. I've got it set with three places and even a candle in the middle.

He looks back at me, and it's like I just know what he's going to say.

"Oh, um, Jade. I'd really like to stay, but I promised Dalma…"

Everything goes blank after that. A week before the spring dance, he has the nerve to say to me, "I promised Dalma." It was like he stuck a knife in my eye. That's what it felt like.

"Fine," I say. I smile because there's no way I'm going to let him know he hurt me, but clearly this has upset Gavin. He wanted Mick to stay too. "You'd better go," I say. "Thank you for your help."

"Don't be like that," he says.

Me! Like I'm the one doing it.

Gavin starts to cry. I stand in front of him and turn to Mick. "Please don't *help* us again. You're the one making him so sick. You know that, don't you?"

Mick

Chapter Seventeen

Dalma looks across the table at me and mouths the word *sorry*. Mrs. Zagar really did serve intestines, but that's not what I'm worried about.

"This is delicious," I say. Dalma's little sister, Flora, whispers to her mother in Croatian. Her mother looks at me and says, "Thank you."

The whole evening pretty much goes like that. Her parents say something to me. One of the kids translates. I say something else. They translate again.

While they're doing that, my mind keeps slipping back to Jade. I still can't believe what happened tonight. All I did was mention Dalma, and she went ballistic.

What was she thinking? She's seen us together for weeks. It's not like we've been hiding anything. I don't think this is just exhaustion. I'm starting to worry there's something really the matter with her.

"You like more?" Mrs. Zagar says without any help.

"Sure," I say and hand her my plate.

"Sure—or yeah, sure? There is difference," says Dalma. She and her sister laugh while her parents try to figure out what's going on.

Flora's laughing makes me think of Gavin. That's who I'm worried about the most. We had a great time at the park this afternoon. He was just like a regular four-year-old, running, jumping, playing with that stuffed kangaroo of his.

Maybe I'm listening to Quinn too much, but I found myself wondering if Gavin really did have a migraine. I asked him about it when we were over by the sandbox. He started filling a little bucket up with sand. He wouldn't look at me. He kept saying he doesn't like magic sprinkles.

I asked him what they were. He put down the bucket, then looked around to see if anyone was there.

He whispered, "I can't tell you."

"C'mon! Give me a hint," I said.

I wasn't sure if this was a game or not. He held Kanga up and whispered in her ear as if she was going to tell him what to say.

"I get them all the time," he said.

"From who?"

He shook his head. He looked scared.

"Gimme another hint?" I gave him a little poke in the belly. "C'mon. Just one more." He talked to Kanga again, then picked up a stick and drew something in the sand.

"M," I said, "for Mick." I taught him how to spell my name.

He drew an *S*.

"And a snake for Staynor!" It's an old joke of ours.

He nodded.

"*I* gave you magic sprinkles?" I said. He really laughed at that. I figured he was playing a trick on me.

That's all he'd say about it until we stopped in the grocery store a little later. We were walking down the spice aisle, and I was talking about buying him a treat, and he got all agitated about magic sprinkles again.

I didn't know what brought that on. It took me forever to calm him down. I had to buy both him and Kanga a banana.

I finish my second helping of intestines and do my best to answer the Zagars' questions. Yes, I have a brother and a sister. Yes, I enjoy hockey and basketball. Yes, my father is an accountant, and my mother stays home. Yes, I want to be an accountant too. (I make that up. I have no idea what I want to be.)

Dalma rushes me out the door as soon as dinner's over. She apologizes for the interrogation, but I didn't mind it. I like her family. They're like her. They don't have all the words yet, but you can tell they're having fun by the look in their eyes.

We walk outside. I can't kiss her because Flora's watching from her bedroom window.

I reach out to shake her hand, and she cracks up. We arrange where we're going to meet tomorrow, then I get in my car and go. It's time I talk to my parents about Jade.

Jade's Diary

Chapter Eighteen

April 26

Gavin won't talk to me. I need to know what he said. He's little. He's got a big imagination. Kids make stuff up all the time. Especially when they're upset. And Mick saw how upset Gavin was. He can't rush in here like a knight in shining armor, then just desert us.

It's time he understood that. It's time he saw how much he's hurting us. Mick's behavior is going to make Gavin very sick.

Mick

Chapter Nineteen

When I get home, my brother and a bunch of his friends are in the kitchen, drinking beer and acting like idiots. I forgot Mom and Dad are out at a dinner party tonight. I'll have to talk to them tomorrow about Jade. I say hey to the guys, then head up to my room. I had this brainwave about what magic sprinkles might be, and I want to check it out.

I google childhood migraines again. Nausea, vomiting, pain, dizziness. That's Gavin, all right. What I'm interested in, though, is the aura. That's what they call this weird thing that happens to people's eyesight right before the headache hits. Different people see different things. It could be bright lights, blobs, zigzag lines, starbursts, sparkles, a big black hole right in the middle of their vision, anything. It's crazy stuff.

I scroll down the page until I find the line I was trying to remember.

Scintillating scotoma—a spot of flickering light near or in the center of the visual field.

That's the medical name for it—but not what you'd call the aura if you were four. You'd probably call it something more like *magic sprinkles*.

That almost makes me happy. At least something makes sense. I even like the way a little kid would turn it into something fancy. It's not a scotoma that's going to give you a killer headache. It's magic sprinkles, like something you'd find in a fairy tale.

I scan the page for more info. I notice the list of foods that can trigger a migraine. I wonder if it's different from the one Jade posted on the kitchen cupboard. She might have missed something.

I scroll down. Pepperoni. Chocolate. Red wine. MSG.

MSG. It jumps right out at me. The initials are MS too.

Yeah, okay. What an amazing coincidence. I keep reading. Caffeine, cheese, artificial sweeteners…but something is bugging me.

I can't remember what Jade said MSG was.

I google it too. Oh, right. That stuff they put in Chinese food. There's a picture. It comes in a spice bottle and looks sort of like salt.

Or sprinkles.

Magic sprinkles.

I think of Gavin starting to cry in the grocery store. We were in the spice aisle. I remember that, because I'd looked around to see what might have set him off. All I'd noticed were bottles of cinnamon and boxes of kosher salt, so I'd figured it had to be something else.

In the park, Gavin had said he got magic sprinkles before. Did he mean he *saw* them before—or that someone *gave* them to him before?

I feel almost as if I'm having an aura myself. The words are kind of floating around on the screen. What I'm thinking doesn't make sense. Jade loves Gavin. She'd do anything for him. She'd never hurt him.

Why don't I believe that anymore?

Mick

Chapter Twenty

I stand outside Jade's apartment building. It's almost midnight. I know it's too late to be here. I key in the security code and open the door to the lobby.

It would be better to talk to her about this tomorrow, when we're both rested and can talk reasonably.

But we're never going to be able to speak reasonably about this. I've got to do it now. I push the elevator button. By tomorrow, she may have done it again.

Done what? I don't even know exactly.

I stare at the numbers above the elevator doors. They're not moving. It's broken again.

I should go home. I never would have thought anything like this if Quinn hadn't planted the idea in my brain. Can I really picture Jade poisoning her little brother?

I take the stairs two at a time.

There's light coming out from under the apartment door. Someone's awake.

I knock.

"Jade." I say it not much louder than a whisper—I don't want to wake the neighbors—but I know she heard me.

"Jade," I say again. "I need to talk to you about something." It hits me that those are the exact words I used to break up with her.

She opens the door a tiny bit and whispers back at me. "It's too late, Mick." Too late for what? My heart is thumping like a punching bag. I picture Gavin lying on the floor.

"No, please," I say. I push past her and into the apartment. I'm like a crazy person.

She grabs my arm. "We're over. You can't come in here in the middle of the night thinking I'll take you back. Now go."

"Where's Gavin?" I say.

"In bed. Where do you think he is?"

"Let me see him."

"No."

"I want to see him." I'm making no attempt to keep my voice down anymore. I walk behind the couch and toward his room.

She beetles around until she's standing in front of me. She's tiny and blond and pretty, and she's the scariest thing I've ever seen.

Her eyes are squinted up, and her lips are pulled together. "You'll give him a migraine," she says.

I look past her and see the kitchen. All the contents of the cupboards have been dumped out on the floor. She goes stiff when she sees me looking. She's too small to block my view.

"I'm not the one giving him the migraines, am I, Jade?"

She's suddenly more alert, as if she's about to give a presentation. She clearly knows what I'm getting at.

"Yes, you are. You upset him. You come and you go. You dump him when he needs you the most. Poor little GooGoo. I don't know how you could be so cruel." She's put on this little-girly tone, and I realize something.

Magic sprinkles aren't Gavin's words. *GooGoo. Put on your jimmy-jams.* Jade's the one who talks like that, not him.

Is that what she told him they were called? Did he catch her doing it? Or did she make it into a game? All part of the fun?

"You've been putting MSG in his food, haven't you?"

"What are you talking about?"

"Magic sprinkles."

"Why would I do that?" She should look more surprised than she does. "He's just making that up. He's little. He makes things up all the time."

"No I don't, Jade."

We turn around. Gavin is standing in the door to his room. His mouth is turned down into a pout, and he's clutching Kanga.

"I don't make things up. I saw you. You give me magic sprinkles. *MS* stands for magic sprinkles and *G* for Gavin."

Jade scurries over and gets down on her knees in front of him.

"Don't tell stories, Gumpy-bear. People may believe you. You'll get Jadie in trouble."

She looks right into his eyes and rubs her hands down either side of his head. She won't hurt him with me here.

"I know my letters, Jade," he says.

She smiles. "Yes, you do, little man. You're very smart. But even smart people make things up sometimes."

"I didn't make it up," he says. He reaches into Kanga's pouch and pulls out a small glass bottle. "See?" He points at the label. "MSG. Just like on the list."

Jade jumps. "Give that to me."

He won't. "I'm sorry I took it, Jadie! I'm sorry. I'm sorry you had to mess up the kitchen." He lies on the bottle like it's a hand grenade.

I'm trying to pull them apart when the door opens and Angie walks in.

Jade's Diary

Chapter Twenty-One

April 30

I don't understand how this could happen. It's a nightmare. No one believes me.

Mick's behind this. He set me up. It would have been so easy for him. He's Gavin's hero. Gavin would believe anything he said. He's only four.

It wouldn't take much to convince him he was being poisoned. Now everyone thinks I'm the crazy one. That's what they're thinking. They've all forgotten how Mick cheated on me. He gets to be the good guy again.

I don't even care about that. All I care about is Gavin. They won't let me see him. I'm worried sick. Who's going to look after him?

Not Mom. She didn't even know how many migraines he was having. That's how much she cares.

Not his dad. He's back now, but how long do you think that's going to last? First time anyone needs money, he'll be gone like a shot.

Not the doctors. I told them there was something the matter with Gavin, but they never did a thing about it. They must be delighted they've got me to blame now.

Not Mick. He's too damn busy with his new girlfriend.

Gavin's going to get really sick without me. Just you watch. They'll be sorry.

Mick

Chapter Twenty-Two

Jade's mother is sitting across from me at McDonald's. She's taken three weeks off work but doesn't look like she's caught up on her sleep yet.

"Shoo! Go play," she says to Gavin. We watch him duck into the fun room. He waves from the slide, then forgets about us and starts talking with a little girl.

Angie says, "That didn't take long." She seems a lot younger when she smiles, but she's never smiled much.

She holds her paper coffee cup in both hands. She pushes the rim up flat with her thumb.

"I don't want you to think badly of her," she says.

I don't say anything.

She puts on a smile for Gavin, who's back at the top of the slide again. "It's my fault," she says. "I was too busy. I gave her too much responsibility. Looking after her little brother. Buying the groceries. Cleaning the apartment. Doing her schoolwork. Shouldering half the worry about money. That's too much. She's only seventeen. She needed looking after herself. A young girl like that needs attention too."

I agree with her there.

"I'm not saying from you, Mick." She keeps playing with her coffee cup. "That wasn't your job. It was mine."

She takes a swig of coffee, but it doesn't stop her lip from quivering.

"That's all this was about. Attention. She just needed attention, and this was the only way she could get it. She's not a bad person."

I'd like to believe that.

"How is she?" I say.

Angie tucks her hair behind her ear. She's wearing a jacket that used to be Jade's. It's gotten kind of shabby, and I feel embarrassed for her.

"She's not happy, but the hospital is good for her. Lets her get some rest and keeps her away from some of the things that could trigger her."

She pushes her donut at me. "Want this? I don't think I'm going to eat it after all."

I almost say, "Save it for Gavin" but remember he can't have chocolate. "Sure," I say.

She takes a breath. "It's called Munchhausen syndrome by proxy, Mick. That's what she's got. It's a psychological condition. Caregivers harm a child in order to get attention for themselves. The doctor said that other than being so young, she's a textbook case."

That almost makes me laugh. It's just like Jade to do it exactly right.

Angie turns her face away and dabs at a tear with her finger.

"I feel so bad," she says. "I should have known something was up after that car accident. It didn't make sense. Gavin said there was no cat. He said she went, *Here goes!* and just turned into the ditch. But who are you going to believe? A teenager who's never, ever done anything wrong or a kid who talks to a stuffed kangaroo?"

She laughs at that, but not for long.

"I didn't know about all those migraines," she says. "I gave the preschool people permission to talk to Jade if there was a problem with anything. The idea was that she'd pass it on to me. She never did, so I just assumed everything was hunky-dory. Gavin was always asleep by the time I got home."

She starts to cry. "I'd never even have known what she was up to if it weren't for you, Mick."

"No," I say. "If it weren't for Gavin, you mean. He's the one who figured it out. He saw MSG on the list and MSG on the label and knew she shouldn't be putting it on his sandwich. He hid the bottle. He's a smart little guy."

I say that to make her feel better, but it only makes her cry more. She takes a napkin and pats her face dry.

"Sorry," I say.

She shakes her head and puts on a perky voice. "We're going to be fine. My parents live in Brockville. We'll go live with them as soon as Jade gets out of the hospital. It'll be a brand-new start for all of us. Just what the doctor ordered. Mom will look after Gavin. Jade can finish high school. And I'll finally take that medical secretary course I've been meaning to take."

She stands up. "It's been nice seeing you, Mick." She gives me a hug, and then she calls Gavin. "C'mon, honey! We've got to go see Jade."

He doesn't even hesitate. He runs right over.

It takes me a long time to explain it all to Dalma. I don't mind.

Vicki Grant has been called "a superb storyteller" by the *Canadian Children's Book News* and "one of the funniest writers working today" by *The Vancouver Sun*. She's written a number of titles in the Orca Soundings series, including *Comeback, Dead End Job* and *I.D.* She lives in Halifax, Nova Scotia. Find out more about her award-winning novels at vickigrant.com.